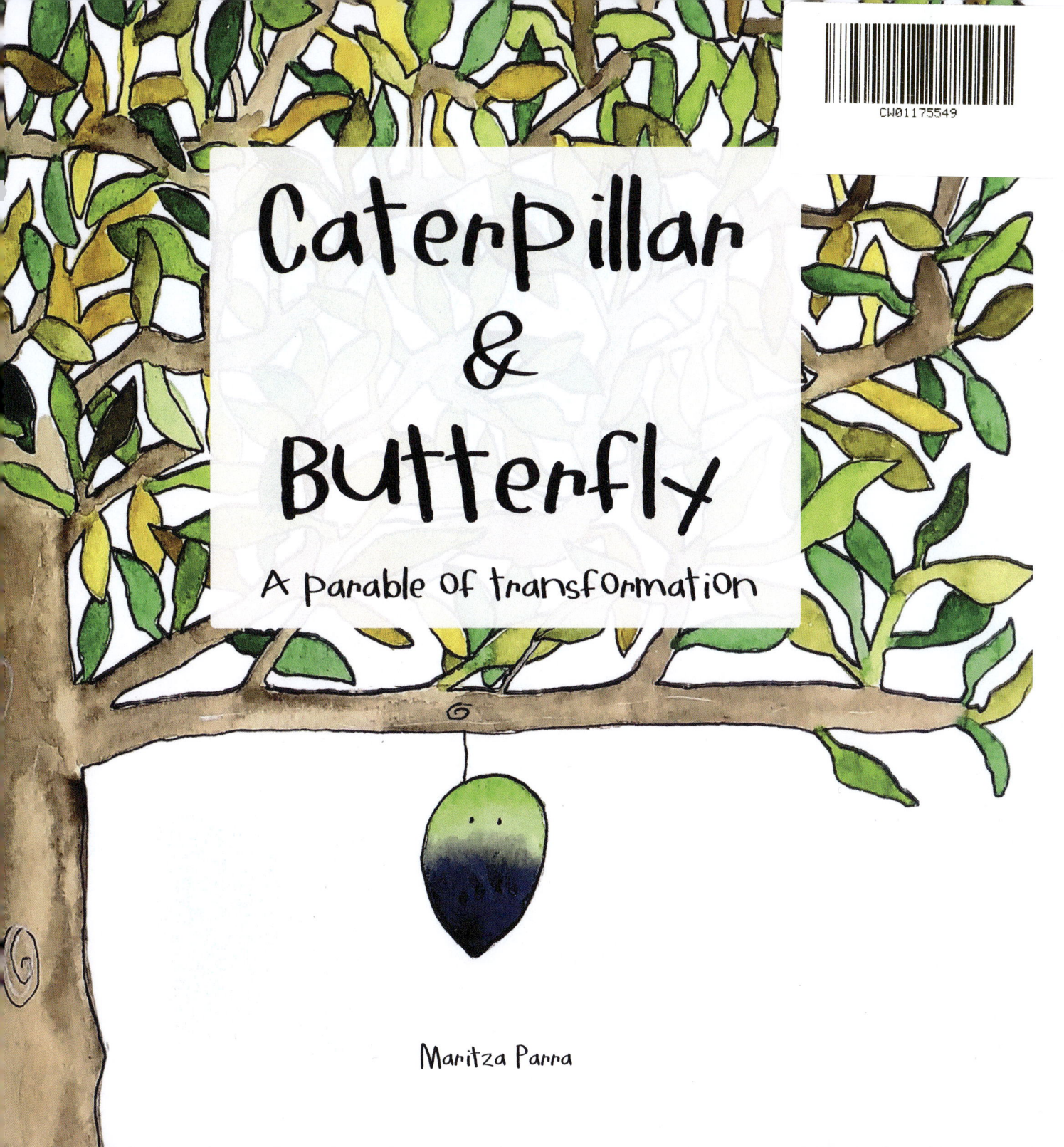

one day...

Get the Heartwork Journaling book on Amazon:
MaritzaParra.com/HWJ-book

© 2020 copyright Maritza Parra | Yuyi Communications LLC
Text and images Maritza Parra © 2020

First published in 2020 by Yuyi Communications LLC

20540 Highway 46W
Suite 115 #290
Spring Branch, TX 78070
Telephone: 210-307-0313

MaritzaParra.com

All rights reserved worldwide.

No part of this book can be reproduced or used in any form or by any means - graphic, electronic, or mechanical, including photocopying, recording, or information-storage-and-retrieval systems without the written permission of the publisher or copyright owners and if said written permission is received, must include author and website attribution to MaritzaParra.com.

The art, illustrations and designs in this book are intended for the personal, non-commercial use of the retail purchaser and are under federal copyright laws; they are not to be reproduced in any form for commercial use. Permission is granted to photocopy content for the personal use of the retail purchaser.

ISBN: 9798670315371

Note:
Any spelling or grammatical errors in the this book are intentional and placed there in a further effort to help us all become perfectionistically sober.

Dedicated to current and future Heartworkers.

Your life matters exactly as it is now...
and as it will be.

Once there was a beautiful caterpillar.

Caterpillar worked hard at being the best, most productive caterpillar.

Caterpillar ate lots and lots and lots of yummy, green leaves.

Caterpillar ate and ate and ate.

No matter how much Caterpillar ate,
it was never enough.

Caterpillar inched far and wide looking for more and more leaves to eat, faster and faster.

One day, Caterpillar felt something strange.

A nudge in the heart.

Caterpillar paused to notice

then kept busy doing what she knew to do.

the heart nudge kept coming back.

Stronger each time.

Uncomfortable.

Unfamiliar.

Insistent.

Caterpillar tried to ignore and resist the uncomfortable feeling.

When the feeling came back
caterpillar got busy, busy, busy looking for more leaves.

Once day, Caterpillar came to drink
from a water droplet in a leaf.

Butterfly landed to drink water too.

"Oh you're so pretty" said Caterpillar

"Thank you" replied Butterfly.

Butterfly sipped water.

Caterpillar sipped water.

Butterfly asked "Have you felt it yet?"

"Felt what?" Caterpillar replied.

"the divine discomfort"
Butterfly whispered with a smile.

"What are you talking about?"
Caterpillar side-eyed.

"Well, there comes a time in most caterpillar's lives where you'll feel an unfamiliar nudge in your heart."

A longing.

A knowing that you're made for more.

Caterpillar stared at Butterfly in wonderment.

"Yes. I have felt it."

Butterfly explained....

"It's an invitation to follow your heart and transform into the next version of you."

Caterpillar felt fear.

"but I'm safe. Comfortable.
I know what I'm doing."

Butterfly soothed Caterpillar.

"You can choose to stay as you are now.
there isn't anything wrong with that."

But if you choose to follow your divine discomfort,
you'll be in for the adventure of a lifetime."

Butterfly wrapped a wing around Caterpillar

"It will take courage."

"You'll have to let go of yourself as you are now

You'll have to look inside

Question who you are now

Question what's possible for you

You'll shed your old identity

Believe brand new thoughts

Feel new feelings

Adopt different behaviors

You'll struggle less and be more."

"I can't tell you the exact process for you because transformation is unique to each Caterpillar."

"Here's what I know for sure...

At the end, you'll still be you

yet a different you
with different possibilities."

Butterfly began to fly away and said....

"If you choose to follow your divine discomfort,
you'll do things that you cannot imagine right now."

If you choose not to follow it,
that uncomfortable feeling in your heart
will never go away."

Caterpillar spent the next days thinking about Butterfly's words.

the divine discomfort grew.

One day, it was so strong that Caterpillar decided to listen.

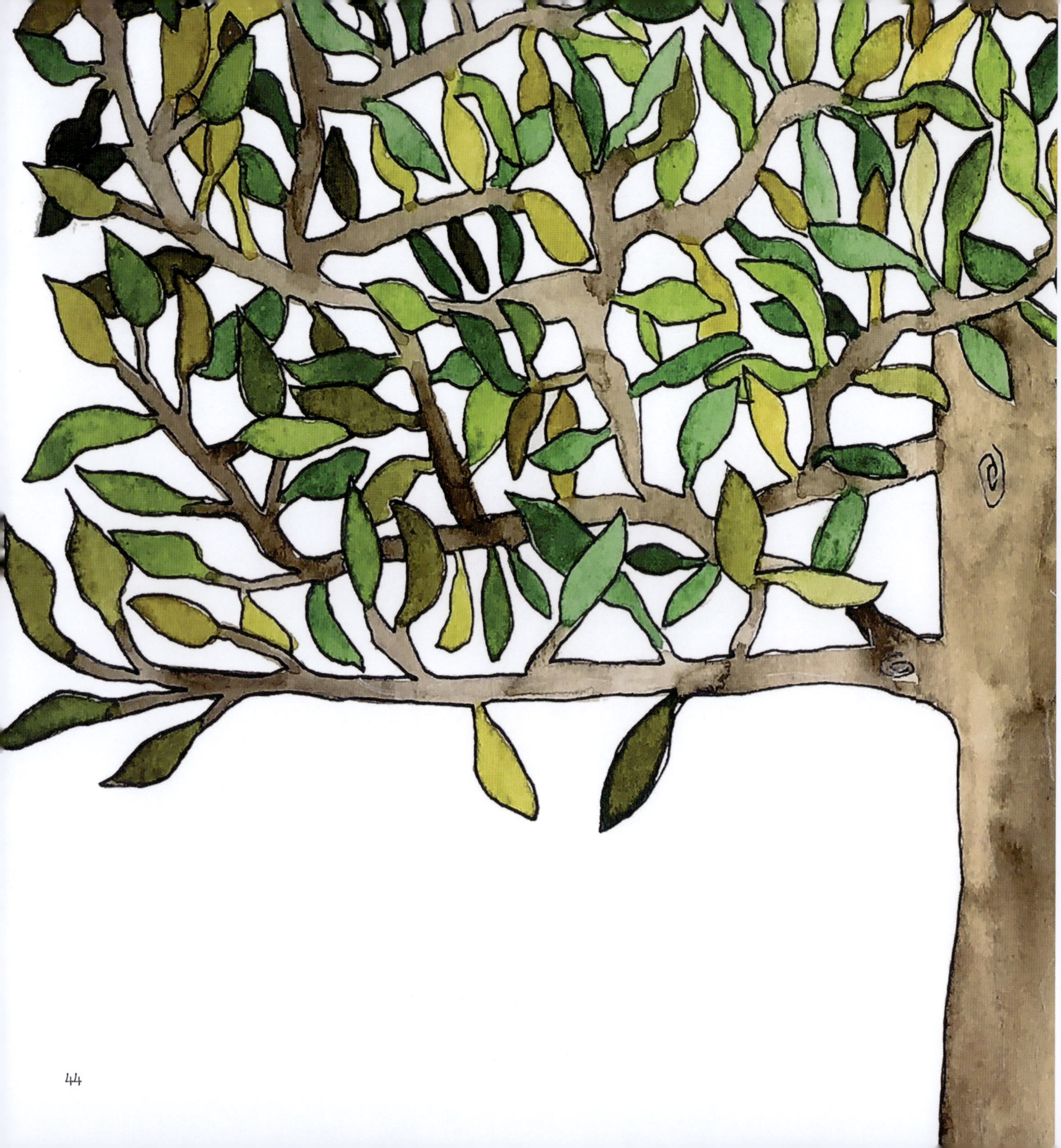

Caterpillar found a safe, quiet place.

And went inside.

It was unfamiliar.

Calm.

Alone.

Caterpillar was present in a brand new way.

Caterpillar saw all the thoughts, beliefs, feelings and behaviors that created this identity.

All of her pieces began to liquify and dissolve.

Caterpillar felt deep self compassion, acceptance and so much love.

Caterpillar chose new thoughts, beliefs, feelings and behaviors to practice on purpose.

Caterpillar knew the constant searching and busyness was over.

those new choices reassembled
into a new version of self.

this chosen new self began to emerge.

Clumsily at first, wings unfolded.

Caterpillar had transformed into a Butterfly.

Slowly Butterfly stretched
new wings and lifted into the air.

Into a whole new world.

with new vision and new possibilities.

As Buttefly started this new adventure,
she realized....

this is who she was meant to be all along.

Butterfly was home.

When people bring their big dreams to get coaching help with, they've usually been struggling to make them happen for a while. It's an honor to help people create the "unrealistic" results that they really want in their lives WHILE not increasing the struggle and overwhelm.

It's a deep mindset shift, but one that results in freedom. Freedom to create more of what you do want. Freedom to let go of the struggle.

Struggle is something I'm well acquainted with too. For decades, I prided myself on a "whatever it takes" Type A, high achiever mentality. Excellence of service can be created with less struggle, more calm, from sufficiency and abundance rather than overwhelm and lack. It's the best way to create it.

Dropping the struggle, dropping the "busyness" has been one of the greatest journeys of my life. I love helping my coaching clients do the same. It's not easy. We've been socialized to be proud of the struggle. But it's easier than we make it.

In the next pages, I'll share some journal prompts that have helped my clients make the switch from struggle to possibility.
With Love and Appreciation,
Maritza

Find me on social:

Instagram.com/themaritzaparra

Facebook.com/LiveYourLifeinFullColor

Pinterest.com/themaritzaparra

Twitter.com/maritzaparra

What do I want to create? _____
_____
_____
_____
_____
_____
_____
_____
_____
_____
_____

How will I feel when I ALREADY have that in my life? (Give a one word answer for the feeling.) _____

What thoughts can I think and practice NOW that help me feel that emotion in my body NOW? _____
_____
_____
_____
_____
_____

Where and how have I been struggling to create this? _____
_____
_____
_____
_____
_____
_____
_____
_____
_____
_____

How do I feel when I'm in the struggle? (Give a one word answer for this feeling.)
_____

Describe how that emotion feels in your body. _____
_____
_____
_____
_____
_____
_____

What's the worst that can happen? _____

_____
_____
_____
_____
_____
_____
_____
_____
_____
_____
_____

What's the best that can happen? _____

_____
_____
_____
_____
_____
_____
_____
_____
_____
_____

Free Stuff

Free online course.

How to Coach Yourself with Heartwork Journaling

Access your inner wisdom, manage your mind and solve any problem.

MaritzaParra.com/5dayseries

What is Heartwork Journaling?

A simple 5 step journaling tool to bring awareness and insight to how your thoughts, emotions and actions work together to create your results.

This tool will help you create everyday mental and emotional health.

No matter what's going on around you.

Learn more at MaritzaParra.com/5dayseries

Maritza Parra is a certified Life Coach, best selling author and creator of Heartwork Journaling.

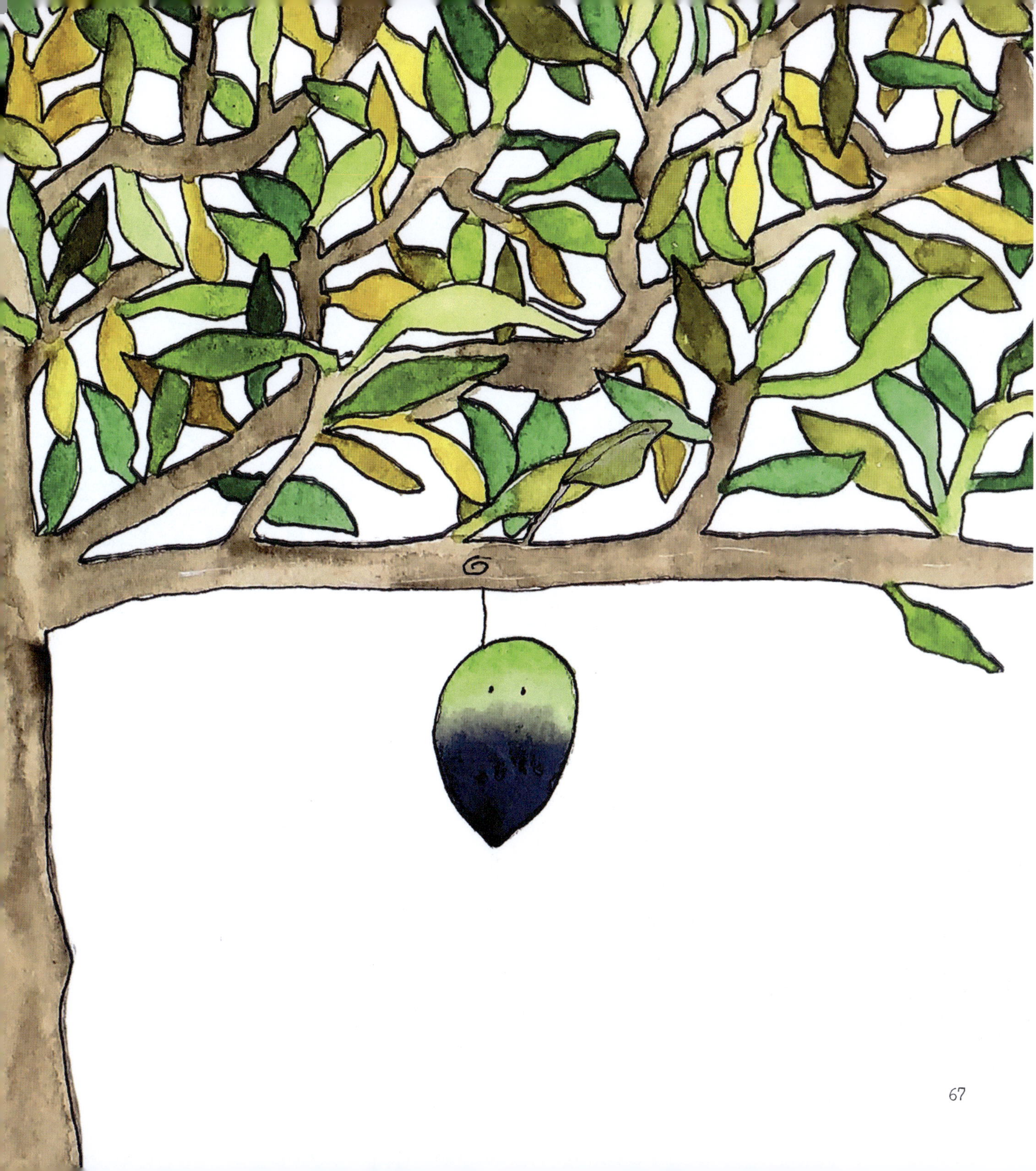

Printed in Great Britain
by Amazon